Dusty

The

Street Sweeper

Story by Charles T. Aguier
Illustrated by Edward S. Barth

D1227659

AuthorHouse™
1663 Liberty Drive
Bloomington, IN 47403
www.authorhouse.com
Phone: 1-800-839-8640

First published by AuthorHouse 2/3/2010

ISBN: 978-1-4490-0544-3 (sc)

Library of Congress Control Number: 2009910789

Printed in the United States of America
Bloomington, Indiana

This book is printed on acid-free paper.

authorHOUSE®

Once upon a time, not too long ago, there was a town called Elmsville. This town had many homes and streets. The streets in Elmsville were very, very clean. So clean that they glistened like gold on a sunny day.

The reason that the streets were so clean was because of Dusty. Dusty was the huge, yellow street sweeper in the town of Elmsville.

Dusty had a driver. His name was Pete. Every morning Pete would take care of Dusty. He would check his oil, fill him with gas, and fill his cleaning tank with water.

Then, Pete would get in Dusty, and away they would go, cleaning the streets of Elmsville. " Over the hills and over the dales, we clean up the streets of Elmsville, without fail," they sang.

The people of Elmsville were so proud of Dusty and Pete for cleaning up the streets. They would line up on the curb and yell, "HIP HIP HOORAY! HIDY HIDY HO! LOOK AT PETE AND DUSTY GO, GO, GO!"

Up and down the streets Dusty and Pete went, day in and day out, singing, " Over the hills and over the dales, we clean up the streets of Elmsville, without fail!"

Then one day Pete took Dusty out to clean the streets. Pete noticed that Dusty was slowing down. "Over the hills and over the dales, we clean up the streets of Elmsville, without fail!" Dusty said. They went up another hill. "Over the hills and over the dales, we clean up the streets of Elmsville, with out fa...."

Dusty broke down. Pete was very, very sad. He called Roger the Repairman on his cell phone. Pete said, "Roger come here quick! I need help! Dusty doesn't run anymore!" Roger replied, "Don't worry, Pete. I'll get a tow truck and maybe we can fix Dusty."

So Roger the Repairman went out with his tow truck. He hooked Dusty up and took Dusty back to the repair shop. Roger told Pete, "Don't worry, Pete. Dusty will be okay. All he needs is a brand new sprocket. Dusty will be all right."

After Roger was done repairing Dusty, Dusty got a full tank of gas. His oil was checked, his cleaning tank was filled with water, and he got a brand new shiny sprocket. Then Pete got in Dusty and away they went, singing, "Over the hills and over the dales, we clean up the streets of Elmsville, without fail!"

Everyone was happy. The people of Elmsville were happy, too. But of all the people, the happiest was Pete. Pete was so proud of Dusty! "Over the hills and over the dales, we clean up the streets of Elmsville, without fail!" they sang together.

All the people of Elmsville yelled, "HIP
HIP HOORAY AND HIDY HIDY HO! LOOK
AT PETE AND DUSTY GO, GO, GO!"
Everyone in Elmsville lived happily ever after.

Dusty the Street Sweeper is dedicated in memory of Tom Tomaselli. A loving husband and caring father. Also a very hard worker who would offer his help whenever he could.

Acknowledgements

Charles T. Aguier would like to thank Mary and Larry Aguier.(thanks Mom and Dad). My wife Janet, and my first grade teacher, Sr. Mary Matthew VSC for teaching me to read. Thank you Edward, for giving Dusty a personality.

Edward S. Barth would like to thank Charlie for his hard work and dedication in the publication of our first book.

Charles and Edward would like to thank Robin Gawlik for her help in putting Dusty together. We would also like to thank all the people, to numerous to mention that helped put our book together. THANK YOU!!!

And finally a special thanks to Thomas and Gregory Aguier. Two fine sons.

E
Aguier, Charles T.
Dusty the street sweeper

Made in the USA
Lexington, KY
10 November 2017